Oscar
Lives Next Door

A Story Inspired by
Oscar Peterson's Childhood

Written by Bonnie Farmer
Illustrated by Marie Lafrance

Daddy is a Pullman porter on the railway. He is dog-tired by the time he gets off the train at Windsor Station. "It's good to be home," he says softly as he lays his head on his pillow. But he doesn't fall asleep, because Oscar lives next door.

Root-a-toot toot goes Oscar's trumpet.
Daddy sits up in bed. **"We're movin',"** he says.
"That Oscar roots and toots too much."

Bing bang bop goes Oscar's piano.

"We're movin'," says Daddy, pulling the pillows up over his ears.
"That Oscar bings, bangs, and bops too much."

Oscar's brothers and sisters play musical instruments, too. They jam day and night!

Bing bang bop-bop-bang root-a-toot toot toot.

"We're movin'," Daddy shouts. **"I can't stand this racket anymore."**
He shoves cotton in his ears, but nothing can drown out the music from next door.
We never do move. I love listening to Oscar's lullaby long after the shuffling, scuffling
noises of our neighborhood hush.

One day, Oscar races me down Atwater Street. We run past the dress shop with its doll-ladies dressed in sparkling gowns. And we sprint past the beauty parlor, where hair sizzles between the hot comb's teeth. My legs are shorter and move faster than Oscar's long legs, but he takes bigger strides than I do. He reaches the corner before me.

"Let's pretend to be elephants," I say. We lumber down the street, swaying our arms from side to side and bellowing.

A farmer's cart rolls by us on its way to the market.

"*Neigh,*" whinnies the horse pulling the cart.

"*Neigh,*" we answer back, bobbing our heads and lifting our feet high like horses.

We giddyup back to the church, where we play a trick on Reverend James. We bang on the church door and hide. Reverend James pokes his head out of a window.

"Oscar! Mildred!" he calls. **"Come out from those bushes!"**

My heart pounds in my chest. Oscar's eyes are as big as saucers. We dash away, squealing like piglets. We don't stop running 'til we're back home. Oscar is laughing so hard he starts to cough. He has to bend over to catch his breath.

Oscar's father calls and points to his watch. It is time for Oscar's music lesson.

"See you tomorrow, Oscar," I say.

Oscar waves good-bye.

On warm evenings, we sit on the back porch listening to neighborhood sounds. A train whistle wails in the distance. Daddy's train.

"That's A and F," says Oscar.

I strain to listen, but only Oscar can hear every musical note of the howling **choo chooooos** as Daddy's train leaves the station and clangs along the canal.

The trumpet is Oscar's favorite instrument.

"There's a genie inside," whispers Oscar. "Listen."

He blows a few notes and, like magic, a turbaned genie curls out of the trumpet's mouth and floats above the telephone wires.

Oscar is a magician.

The following Saturday morning, I wait for Oscar to race me to the corner again, but he doesn't come out. I knock on his door.

"Is Oscar home?" I ask.

"Oscar's very sick, dear," replies Mrs. Peterson. "He had to go to the hospital last night."

It turns out Oscar has a disease with a long name. TU-BER-CU-LO-SIS. Thank goodness there is a shorter way to say it: TB. Oscar has TB. The doctor says he'll get better, but it will take a long time.

I hide in the hall closet.

"Millie!" Mom calls me to supper. I squirm deeper into the closet. "Mildred, what are you doing?"

"We played a trick on Reverend James. Is that why Oscar's sick?"

Mom smiles and shakes her head. "No, Millie, you catch TB from other people, not from making mischief. It's like a really, really bad cold. It hurts your chest and makes you cough a lot."

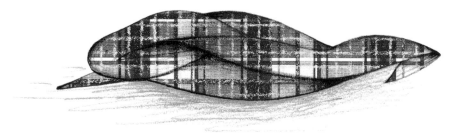

Mama rings Mrs. Peterson's doorbell and invites her over for tea.

"How is Oscar?"

Mrs. Peterson stirs her tea a moment, then blurts, "He won't talk! We can't get a peep out of him. He *refuses* to talk. The nurses are beside themselves. His father thinks he needs a good spanking. What shall we do? I'm at the end of my rope."

I can't visit him in the hospital, so I make Oscar a card.

Dear Oscar,

The trick we played on Reverend James did not make you sick. Get better and come home soon.

Love, Millie
XOXOXOXOXOXO

I draw a picture on the envelope and seal it. Mom and I trudge
up the hill to the children's hospital and give it to the nurse at the
front desk.

"He'll be thankful for a kind gesture from a friend," she says.

I wait a long, lonesome time for Oscar to get better.

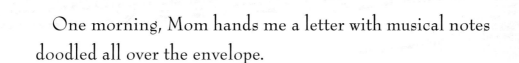

One morning, Mom hands me a letter with musical notes doodled all over the envelope.

Dear Millie,

I got a tractor. It's red and silver and big as a house. The nurses gave it to me because I am so quiet. I like it here now. I was scared and lonely before. I wish you were here too.

Oscar
XO

Not long afterward, Mrs. Peterson tells Mom that Oscar's talking and laughing again.

"He's back to his old self," she says. And I'm glad.

Spring breezes blow fat bellies into Mama's washing, and Oscar is still in the hospital.

At nighttime, I toss and turn. Without Oscar's lullaby, I can't fall asleep. I tiptoe into the living room where Daddy listens to the radio, and I curl up on the carpet like a cat. Soft jazz plays through the radio's carved wooden panel. I believe Daddy misses Oscar, too.

When Daddy falls asleep, I wander out to the back porch. A light is on at Oscar's. I peek through the kitchen window and see him hunched over the piano. His fingers tickle the keys while the radio **purrs smoky rhythms**.

Oscar is home.

The next day, Oscar stands on the back porch holding his trumpet. He puts it to his mouth and gently presses the keys, but no sound comes out.

Daddy and I watch as Oscar takes apart his horn, bit by bit, piece by piece. **"I want to see where the magic comes from,"** he says.

He pokes a finger inside the brass tubes. He looks through one end like a ship's captain. Pretty soon, the floor is cluttered with shiny tubes and valves that he can't put back together. Oscar looks like he might cry.

Daddy tells me that Oscar's lungs are no longer strong enough to blow into a horn.

Daddy tips his porter's cap and kisses me good-bye. "When I get back to Montreal, I want to see smiles on both of your faces."

I sit beside Oscar on the porch. Warm rain **pitter-patters** on Oscar's scattered horn. I pick up one of the shiny tubes.

"Maybe there's a genie inside the piano, too," I say.

We stand on chairs, open the top of the piano, and gaze inside.

Rows of little wooden hammers wearing felt hats run from one side of the piano to the other. Bands of wires stand at attention in front of the hammers.

We take turns playing a key and watching the little hammer strike the wire.

Oscar sits at the piano. His fingers pause over the keys for a moment before playing. When they finally touch the keyboard, it sounds like **rolling thunder.**

His father hires a piano teacher, and Oscar practices,

practices,

practices.

We don't have as much time to play anymore, but we still like to sit on the back porch. Tonight, Mama has a treat for Oscar and me, but it's not ready yet. We watch the sun set while jazz music bubbles up from a dance club.

"I'm gonna be an explorer," says Oscar.

"I'm gonna be a ballerina," I say.

We daydream while Mama's cornbread cools on the windowsill.

Author's Note

I'd always wanted to write a children's book about growing up in Little Burgundy. The area means a great deal to me. It was where my mother and I settled after moving to Montreal from Nova Scotia. I attended the Montreal Day Nursery and later crossed the railway tracks every day to get to Royal Arthur School. Hot lunches were served at the Negro Community Centre (NCC) for ten cents a day. And then there was the Union United Church, a hub of social and religious activity for the neighborhood's diverse population of blacks from Canada, the Caribbean, and the US. It was a neighborhood of corner stores, steep spiraling staircases, stoops, and lines of washing—all hemmed in by two railway lines, the Canadian National Railway (CN) and the Canadian Pacific Railway (CP).

I'd been thinking a long time about Little Burgundy when I came up with the idea of writing about the boy who became the neighborhood's most well-known resident—Oscar Peterson. In Oscar's childhood, Little Burgundy was known as St-Henri. Decades before I lived there, Oscar crossed the same railway tracks to attend the same elementary school as I did. His father, like so many black men in the neighborhood, worked as a porter on those railways. Later, his sister Daisy taught piano at the NCC to countless young people.

In this story, I've tried to blend fiction with non-fiction. Millie is fictitious and so are some of the antics she and Oscar get up to. But her chronicles of Oscar's bout with tuberculosis, his selective mutism, his sense of loss over not being able to play the horn, and his ultimate deep appreciation of the piano are all true.

Oscar's whole family was musical. His mother, Kathleen, sang while his father, Daniel, played piano and encouraged all his children to be musicians. Oscar had four siblings. Fred played piano. Charles played piano and trumpet. May also played piano. Daisy, who played both trombone and piano, was one of Oscar's first piano teachers.

When Oscar was seven, he caught tuberculosis (TB), a frightening disease that infects the lungs, and for which, at that time, there was no real cure other than isolation and bed rest. Tuberculosis was so contagious that several members of the same family often caught it, which was the case in Oscar's family. His sister Daisy was hospitalized, as was his brother Fred, who eventually died from the disease. Oscar had to be hospitalized for more than a year until his lungs healed. Being away from his family must have been a scary, confusing time for little Oscar because, for a short while, he stopped talking. A gift of a toy tractor from a charity helped him find his voice again.

Although Oscar's illness weakened his lungs, it did not affect his perfect pitch. Oscar could recognize the musical notes of any sound. When he was in high school, Oscar won a piano contest at CBC Radio. He started playing piano in Montreal jazz clubs. Many of these clubs, such as the Alberta Lounge, were near his Little Burgundy neighborhood.

Not long afterward, his musical career took off, and he traveled all over the world playing all kinds of music. He played classical music, which is played on instruments rather than sung and is listened to rather than danced to. He played boogie-woogie, which is a fast, thumping kind of music that makes you want to tap your toes and dance. And he played jazz. In jazz music, each musician takes a turn playing a tune his or her own way.

Oscar became so famous that he won scores of awards, including several Grammys, recognizing his great musical talent. Some of the musicians Oscar grew up listening to eventually became his friends and musical colleagues. He played with jazz greats such as Dizzy Gillespie, Stan Getz, and Count Basie, and he often accompanied singers such as Billie Holiday and Ella Fitzgerald. In 1972, he received the Order of Canada. His photograph has appeared on a Canadian stamp, and Queen Elizabeth II unveiled a statue of him during her visit to Canada in 2010.

Oscar died on December 23, 2007. Although much of the neighborhood where he grew up is gone forever, demolished in the construction of the Ville-Marie Expressway in the 1970s, Oscar's legacy lives on in the students and jazz enthusiasts who have been influenced by his music, and in his role in putting Montreal and Little Burgundy on the map of jazz history.

Oscar at a piano with his sister Daisy.

For my mother, Phyllis Marina Farmer—B.F.

To my mother, Madeleine, who, in another era, ventured
to Rockhead's Paradise to hear jazz—M.L.

Sources

Archambeau, Gerald A. "A Porter's Pride." *The Hamilton Spectator*, December 4, 2007.

Eng, David. *Burgundy Jazz*. Web documentary. Producer Katarina Soukup. Montreal: Catbird Productions, 2013. Accessed August 8, 2014. http://music.cbc.ca/burgundyjazz

In the Key of Oscar. DVD. Directed by William R. Cunningham and Sylvia Sweeney. Montreal: National Film Board of Canada, 1992.

Kerr, Mark. "Where Have All the Good Jazz Clubs Gone?: The Past and the Golden Era of Montreal Jazz." *The McGill Tribune*, November 25, 2003.

Lees, Gene. *Oscar Peterson: The Will to Swing*. New York: Cooper Square Press, 1988.

The N.C.C.—Charles H. Este Centre. "How It All Started…" Accessed March 13, 2015. http://jasonaltidor.com/ncc/history.php

Peterson, Oscar. *A Jazz Odyssey: The Life of Oscar Peterson*. Editor Richard Palmer. London; New York: Continuum, 2002.

Peterson, Oscar, "Place St. Henri," in *Canadiana Suite*, Limelight Records, 1964.

Ulaby, Neda. "Jazz Piano Master Oscar Peterson Dies." NPR, December 24, 2007. Accessed February 16, 2015. http://www.npr.org/templates/story/story.php?storyId=17587235

Windsor Mosaic. "Brotherhood of Sleeping Car Porters." Accessed February 16, 2015. http://www.windsor-communities.com/african-labour-brotherhood.php

Text © 2015 Bonnie Farmer
Illustrations © 2015 Marie Lafrance

Owlkids Books acknowledges the financial support of the Canada Council for the Arts, the Ontario Arts Council, the Government of Canada through the Canada Book Fund (CBF) and the Government of Ontario through the Ontario Media Development Corporation's Book Initiative for our publishing activities.

Published in Canada by
Owlkids Books Inc.
10 Lower Spadina Avenue
Toronto, ON M5V 2Z2

Published in the United States by
Owlkids Books Inc.
1700 Fourth Street
Berkeley, CA 94710

Library and Archives Canada Cataloguing in Publication

Farmer, Bonnie, 1959-, author
Oscar lives next door : a story inspired by Oscar Peterson's childhood / written by Bonnie Farmer ; illustrated by Marie Lafrance.

ISBN 978-1-77147-104-6 (bound)

1. Peterson, Oscar, 1925-2007--Childhood and youth--Juvenile fiction. I. Lafrance, Marie, illustrator II. Title.

PS8561.A726O23 2015   jC813'.6   C2014-908452-8

Library of Congress Control Number: 2015900228

Edited by: Jennifer Stokes and Karen Li
Designed by: Alisa Baldwin
Photo credit (page 31): Library and Archives Canada / e011073127

Manufactured in Shenzhen, Guangdong, China, in April 2015, by WKT Co. Ltd.
Job #14CB3472

A   B   C   D   E   F

Publisher of Chirp, chickaDEE and OWL
www.owlkidsbooks.com

5/18